Hazardous and Other Stories

Femdom Mind Control

Flash Fiction – Vol. 32

S.B.

Table of Contents

The real danger is not surrendering.

Thank you to all patrons of Spell... B-O-U-N-D.

Cold Revenge

Ashley Hansen opened her eyes to familiar surroundings, enshrouded in darkness. The private room in the back of her house was her sanctum of fetish, a place where no one was allowed inside without an invitation. It was a large, rectangular division dominated by a giant curved screen that had seen many commands of her come to life. However, the messages now displayed there in bright red came from someone else, a stranger whose intents remained unknown.

The thirty-four-year-old faux redhead sat in a silver chair that was freezing to the touch. Her clothes - a white tank top and a pair of rugged jeans - were shredded, needle marks visible on her right arm and left leg. The tissue around them was swollen, purple protuberances against a fair skin. The drugs in her system were still fresh, and so was the haziness clouding her amber-colored eyes. Struggling to move, she faced the screen and read,

"Welcome back, Ashley. Comfortable? Not too much, I hope."

Ashley said nothing, eyes roving the room, looking for her assailant. A vague outline by the door caught her attention. It was of another woman, holding a tablet. She was petite in stature and had slightly Asian traits. It didn't appear to be anyone she knew.

"Keep your eyes on the screen," the mysterious figure said.

"Why, if I already know you're there? What's the point of this charade?"

"I could ask you the same thing. Isn't this the way you love to fuck other people's minds?"

"You must be confusing me with someone else."

"I wish that were true."

The stranger tapped the laptop and five pictures appeared on the main screen. An old man with an anchor-shaped birthmark on his left cheek; a violet-haired young woman with more piercings than flesh left in her right ear; another man, this one dressed in a gray suit and holding a real estate agency business card; a second woman, older than the first and with a fairly average face except for the fact she had a blue eye and a brown one; and finally, another woman, this one in her late twenties and dressed in a flight attendant's uniform. She, too, had oriental features as well as a disarming smile.

"Do any of them look familiar to you, Ashley?" the screen asked.

"No. I've never seen any of them before."

"Are you really just going to sit there and lie?"

"Is that what you think I'm doing?"

"I'm sure of it. You have no secrets from me. I know what you did to all of them, and I say: no more! Your realm of abuse ends tonight."

The stranger touched the laptop again, and the pictures faded into a mesh of black and white interconnected spirals that filled the room.

"What are you doing?"

"Giving you a taste of your own medicine, of course! Was it fun to brainwash them all against their will? It must have been otherwise you wouldn't have kept on doing it. I'm sure you'll love what comes next"

"Wait! We can talk about this, reach some sort of agreement..."

"No, we can't. You lost any chance you had the moment you started kidnapping people to satisfy your lust... And you really shouldn't have fucked with my sister."

The dulling geometrical patterns exploded all around, slowly taking root inside Ashley's thoughts. The indoctrination process was as quick or as slow as anyone wanted it to be. Hers would be the slowest and most painful of all.

Fresh Thoughts

"Dave? Are you there?" Luke asked as he entered his friend's garage, the place where he spent most of his free time, tinkering with everything at hand. He had always had a bit of an inventor side, not quite "mad scientist" material though some of his creations were definitely outside the norm. One of them was probably the reason he had texted him so late that night, urging him to come over. If not, then what else?

"Dave? What is so important that couldn't wait until morning? I need to get some sleep, dude!"

"You'll see," Dave replied, his voice sounding like it was coming from far, far away. "This is wonderful!"

"It better be," Luke negotiated a path between Dave's old motorcycle, now nothing more than a haven of parts for some of his mechanical horrors and piles of cardboard boxes that had seen better days. His friend's voice led him away from the garage and into the connecting hallway that led to the basement of the house. "Damn it!" he muttered as he descended the steep stairs into darkness.

Luke hated basements. They were the bread and butter of his nightmares, with their dusty atmosphere, creepy crawlers, and cobwebs everywhere. Dave's place was no exception, for he hardly ever went to the trouble of cleaning it. An intense odor he couldn't identify clang to his nostrils and stayed there, adding to the extreme discomfort he was already experiencing. Luke gulped and pushed on until he reached the center of the division.

Dave sat straight ahead, back turned to him and facing what appeared to be a freshly dug hole in the lateral foundation of the house. A viscous goo whose color laid somewhere between dark blue and black dripped from it, carrying the same disturbing stench.

"There you are!" Luke exclaimed. "Care to tell me what the fuck is going now?"

"I found a miracle," Dave replied, rotating his chair to meet his friend's horrified gaze. Something bulbous had latched on to his neck, darkening the veins around it. It pulsated with a sickening light, like a beacon of endless destruction.

"FUCK! What is that disgusting thing?" Luke instinctively looked around the basement to find something he could use as a weapon but found nothing.

"Don't speak like that about my Goddess," Dave stood up and growled. His eyes were reddened, and his fingernails covered in fresh blood. The excessive sweat on his forehead and cheeks showed that his bodily temperature was off the charts.

"Goddess?"

"Yes. My owner, my everything! I told you Roxanne would come back one day to take control of my life and now she has. We will never be apart again."

"Roxanne?" Luke scrambled on his feet, trying to make sense of what he was saying. "Your crazy ex that was into bondage? What does she have to do with that... Oh! You're hallucinating, aren't you? Whatever that thing around your neck is, it's messing with your brain."

Dave inched forward, stiff arms and legs ready for a fight to the death if needed be, and said, "I told you not to speak like that again. Apologize to my Goddess now!"

"Okay, easy now. Easy... Just calm down, Dave. There's no reason to get all riled up. Let's talk about this,"

"I didn't call you here to talk, Luke."

"Why did you call me then? What is that you want?"

"Me? Nothing. It was Goddess that insisted I texted you. Thank you for coming. She wants you to have your own personal miracle, too."

"She wants...? Oh, fuck no!" Luke turned around and ran up the stairs, trying to escape the creepy madness he had been unwillingly entangled in. A puddle of good crept at his feet, making slip and fall back into the pit, in time to see another entity descend onto his face, thousands of minuscule suckers protruding from its gelatinous core. The drugs it produced shot quickly into his system, rendering him numb. In time, it would access its memories to find the one idea capable of keeping him in a perpetual blissful sedated state where it was a car, a trip to a tropical island, or a latex-clad BDSM Goddess that loved pain above pleasure. Whatever it turned out to be, Luke would never escape the narcotic dream.

If the infant alien slug feeding off him had a mouth, it would surely be smiling. Fresh thoughts were the best.

Hazardous

"Alpha Leader, this is Charlie Echo. We have eyes on the subject. I repeat, we have eyes on the subject. Shall we proceed with the capture right away?"

"Negative, Charlie Echo," General Masters replied from the sanctity of the command center. "The reinforcements are still being deployed. You are to wait until they contact you and only then can you proceed. Do you copy?"

"Copy, Alpha Leader. We'll continue to monitor the situation from here."

It was a tense Friday morning in the headquarters of Project Monolith, one out of three US specialized divisions in dealing with meta-human threats. After almost a year of complete radio silence, the criminal code named "Hazard" had once again resurfaced and capturing her was not only a priority, but a necessity.

Of the other twelve men and women standing with the General in the underground circular room, eleven agreed with his strategic decision to wait for reinforcements. Only Hank Winters, Washington's latest suit with a bureaucratic mind, showed his discontentment.

"Why are you being so cautious, General?" He asked. "You already have fifty men on location to capture a single woman. How many more do you need?"

"As many as it takes, Mr. Winters," the balding military chief with eagle eyes replied. 'Hazard' isn't an ordinary woman, or didn't you read the reports I sent you?"

"I did," Hank yawned, "but frankly, they all seem like something straight out of a tabloid instead of official documents. She can't be that bad!"

"You're right... she's worse! Underestimating her will only lead to senseless destruction. I'm not making the same mistakes again."

"No, it seems you are intent on making a bunch of new ones. If she's so dangerous, why didn't you mobilize all your efforts to track her down all this time?"

"We did... something that was in the reports, too," the older man spat. "If you're done for the moment, I have better things to do than to put up with your crap right now."

"Whatever... but know that I'm going straight to the President as soon as the operation is over. I'm sure he'll love to hear how Project Monolith is being run so inefficiently right now."

"Do as you must and so will I," the General consulted the position of the incoming reinforcements on the three-dimensional map before him and sighed.

Hazard. Her green and black suit latex suit with the biological material sign highlighted in the front and back only told a portion of her story. No one knew for sure if the radiation she exuded was born of a natural mutation or the result of another agency's research into biological weapons. "Plausible deniability" was always at work when something went south and that applied to the bowels of the government as well. Whatever the truth was, prolonged exposure to her was the most dangerous form of addiction of all.

"Alpha Leader, this is Charlie Echo reporting. We do not have eyes on the subject! I repeat, we do not have eyes on the subject!" a distressed voice suddenly took hold of the veteran's ears.

"Alpha Leader here. Could you repeat that, Charlie Echo? What happened?"

"It's a decoy, Sir. The subject we've been tracking all this time has now been confirmed as nothing more than an elaborate holographic projection. Hazard is not here, General! We don't know where she is!"

"Then why don't I tell you?" a giggle echoed across the Control Room. The General cocked his head and saw a long-haired blonde open the bulk doors as if they were made of paper. Behind her, trailed a regiment of lovesick drones, helplessly poisoned by her charms. "I hope you don't mind I walked right in and if you do, well... you won't worry about that for long."

Guns on the ready, her soldier toys secured the room as she began consuming everyone's desires one by one.

Hank Winters was the first to fall, avid tongue feasting on her latex-clad ass. The General came last after already witnessing the degradation of everyone else. The foul radiation spread across the base, leaving no soul unturned.

Memories of Josie

Patrick closed the attic's door and returned to his living-room, carrying an old wood box. Inside, were all the things that reminded him of Josie, the one that got away. It was a treasure trove of beautiful memories he loved to lose himself in whenever he was feeling down and while his therapist kept saying it was unhealthy to constantly revisit the past, it were those fragments that drove away the dark clouds hovering his mind. He needed the release yet again.

He sat on the leather sofa, next to his twelve-year-old Birman, and opened the box. The fluffy cat raised his head slightly to look at him, saw there was no food in waiting, and went back to sleep with a gentle purr. Patrick smiled at his predictable behavior and examined the contents one by one.

There was a dried sunflower from their first walk together; a movie stub from the only horror movie he had seen in 3-D; a flowery handkerchief that brought him back to the restaurant where he had proposed; the broken pendant with which she used to hypnotize him when she was feeling mischievous...

Once, they had it all. They were the power couple everyone envied and talked about, bound by something greater than the laws of attraction and what was commonly called 'love'. No one expected them to ever break up, yet they did, and to the day he had never fully understood why.

Work? Different priorities? A desire to leave and explore other things while they were still young? Too many possibilities, all left unexplored. The one time communication simply had to work had failed them. He remembered the license plate of the cab that drove her to the airport and nothing more.

Patrick closed his eyes and sighed. It hurt, but the pain was cathartic and always made him feel stronger in the end. He imagined she was sitting where his dozed off and heard her ask,

"You really miss the times we had together, don't you?"

"Yes. I miss them every day. I miss you, Josie."

"What if I told you there was a way to get them back?"

"I would love that, but there isn't. I've tried to reach you. You never answered. I know now you'll never will."

"Never say never, my dear. Open your eyes."

As if a beam of sunlight had descended over his closed eyelids, he blinked and immediately shook his head in disbelief. Josie was where he had hoped she would be, and she hadn't aged a day in fifteen years.

"Hi," she said.

"You're here. You're really here!" he gasped.

"Yes, I am. Surprised?"

"Of course! Oh, my God! It's so good to see you again, but how did you get in?"

"Can you believe that, after all these years, I found out I still had a key to this place? It was in the back pocket of my orange coat. I never wore it again since the day I..."

"... left."

"Yes, and the moment I found it, everything came back to me. It was a remote chance, but I knew where I needed to be. I'm sorry for barging in but I saw you through you the window and you didn't answer the bell, so..."

"I didn't?"

"No. You were so peaceful sitting there with your eyes closed. If I didn't know better, I'd say you were in a trance, sweetie. Do you still do that? Go under, thinking of me?"

"I... I don't know. I suppose that's possible..."

"Good," she rubbed his right cheek with her pearly hands. "I missed you too, Patrick."

"As lovely as it is that you're here, what do you want, Josie? It's been a lifetime already."

"I know. Perhaps, there can be another if you're willing to listen."

"Listen to what?"

"To whatever you wish to hear," she reached for the box and held the broken pendant between her fingers.

"Memories are a powerful thing, and we have plenty of our own. How about we have dinner tonight, we finally talk about them and then, if things work out, we consider making new ones?"

"In trance?"

"In and out of it, for better and worse. We have a lot of catching up to do. We should start right now."

The pendant swung before his already drooping eyes. Her hypnotic charms remained as powerful as ever, filling his heart with everlasting possibilities. He laid down the box at her feet and looked ahead for the first time.

New Religion

Hank's jaw dropped when he entered the cathedral's doors and saw a dozen latex-clad nuns waiting for him. He was dreaming. He had to be for only in dreams and porn movies do such unexpected encounters occur, and he was sure he hadn't been invited to be in the latter. As he thought of what to say in face of such stunning fetish beauties, one of them took the initiative and cooed,

"Hello, wayward sheep. Have you come to confess your sins? I'm afraid we're the only ones here right now and we're not exactly the most qualified people to grant absolution to anyone. However, there's something we can give you... if you're willing to listen..."

The twelve women surrounded him and held hands, creating a circle of power that made his cock immediately hard. It was the first time since forever that such an exciting fantasy came his way, and he was sure to make the best of it while it lasted.

"Damn right I am!" he exclaimed.

The nun giggled at his blasphemy and continued, "What we're offering you is a chance to finally let go of dreadful concepts and traditions. In case, you didn't know it already, Heaven and Hell are nothing more than mythological designs created to control the masses. They're not real, so why should we conform ourselves with the outdated words of a dusty book when it's so much better to enjoy life's little pleasures without worrying about a possible punishment in the afterlife. God and the Devil? As fake as everything else. The only truth lies in the principles of lust, and salvation is found when you surrender your body to it. Don't you want to be free?"

"What do you want me to do, baby?"

"Drop to your knees and pray at the only altar that matters. Become a slave to your passions and succumb to your desire to be owned. You want to be totally controlled by us and we'll grant you that wish. Say goodbye to the outside world and embrace this new way of looking at religion. Let us inside your mind."

All the nuns smiled in unison, sparks of electricity flowing through their interlocked fingers. An otherworldly light shone across the stained-glass windows above Hank's head and descended into the center of the circle momentarily blinding him. In this new world of creeping shadows, he saw the true nature of the creatures trying to claim his soul, demons with piercing eyes, red tails and hissing teeth.

"No!" he exclaimed. "Begone, tempting beasts! You won't get me."

"It's a little too late for that," the leader of the supernatural creatures growled, the enchanted circle strengthening. "You're already too aroused, feeding our power. Feel yourself growing hornier, weaker, and submissive. We will free you from the absurdity of free will and you'll be our nourishment for centuries."

"I want to wake up," he muttered to himself. "Hank, snap out of it right now!"

The circle grew tighter and tighter, rings of pure malice enveloping his arms and legs. They compressed his bones, made the veins in his face pop up. Ravenous clawed hands ripped the latex fantasies into shreds until only the abominations remained, hellbent on devouring him whole.

It was only a dream, yet one he would never wake up from. Hank's neighbors heard him scream in his bedroom at the witching hour, and then there was nothing but deafening silence.

Six months later, he's still missing. The police investigation on his disappearance produced no evidence except one small thing that remains unexplained. At the foot of his bed, the CSI discovered a shredded piece of black latex with a distinctive sulfur smell. Every time they look at it, they can almost see a screaming reflection in the distance.

Not Important Right Now

Ted: God, I'm so excited!

Monica: First time?

Ted: No, I've been excited lots of times.

Monica: I understood that reference.

Ted: Good. *Airplane!* is one of my favorite movies.

Monica: Really? What do you like about it?

Ted: How absurd it is, for starters. I have a knack for nonsense humor. I also like how there's a gag in pretty much every scene, some in the foreground, others in the background. Blink and you miss them. It's a silly movie through and through, but with many layers to it, if you know what I mean.

Monica: I believe so. Hypnosis can be like that too, and that's one reason I love it so much. Just curious: if *Airplane!* is one of your favorite movies, how many times have you seen it already?

Ted: Not sure.

Monica: Five?

Ted: No. More.

Monica: Ten then?

Ted: More than that, too.

Monica: Surely no more than twenty.

Ted: You'd be surprised... and don't call me Shirley!

Monica: I knew you would say that.

Ted: Why?

Monica: Someone who loves the movie so much wouldn't resist the setup to one of its most quotable lines.

Ted: So, you led me on, huh?

Monica: Isn't that what you expect from a hypnotist?

Ted: I suppose though I'm still waiting. When are we doing this?

Monica: Doing what?

Ted: When are you going to hypnotize me, Monica? People keep telling me you're one of the best in the business. It would be nice to know what they're talking about.

Monica: Please, be patient. Whatever needs to happen will do so when you least expect it. Besides, I love to chat with all new clients for a bit to break the ice. Can we keep doing that?

Ted: Sure.

Monica: Glad to hear it. You said you love movies with nonsense humor. Any other favorites besides Airplane!, Ted?

Ted: Of course.

Monica: Name me the first three that come to mind.

Ted: Hmmm... *Blazing Saddles*, *Top Secret!*, and *The Naked Gun*.

Monica: Interesting. I love the first and the last you mentioned, but I don't think I've ever seen the second one. Can you tell me what's it about?

Ted: You've never seen *Top Secret!*? You're missing out big time then. It's basically a parody of Elvis Presley musicals, and spy and World War II films. It tells the story of an American rock star that travels to East Germany and gets entangled in a plot to stop the Germany reunification under a Nazi-like regime. Lots of music numbers but lots of silliness as well. It's great!

Monica: That sounds familiar. Is that the one with Val Kilmer?

Ted: Yeah.

Monica: Cool. It's all coming back to me now. Remember the cow scene?

Ted: How could I forget? Poor Nigel.

Monica: I thought he liked what happened to him.

Ted: He did, but I wouldn't.

Monica: What if it were a woman fucking your ass instead of a bull?

Ted: I still wouldn't have liked it.

Monica: Are you sure about that? Perhaps you could learn to love it.

Ted: Nah, I'm good.

Monica: One day, you'll think differently.

Ted: That's never going to happen.

Monica: If you say so... What do you feel like doing now?

Ted: That hypnosis thing would be nice.

Monica: Going into trance for me?

Ted: Yes.

Monica: Dropping so deep you would find yourself craving things you never craved before and even imagining you're an entirely different person altogether?

Ted: Can you do that?

Monica: I already did and now it's time for you to... *snap* Wake up. Back to your old self. Remember what you wish to remember. Let go of everything else you don't want to keep. Talk to me again when you're ready. I'll be waiting.

(...)

Josh: Monica?

Monica: Yes, Josh?

Josh: How long have you been online?

Monica: About an hour.

Josh: Okay. Hmmm,... were we talking in the meantime?

Monica: We sure were, it was quite the funny conversation.

Josh: What did we talk about?

Monica: Some of your favorite movies. I had no idea you loved *Airplane!* so much.

Josh: What? I've never seen that movie!

Monica: You didn't?

Josh: No! I can't stand that type of crazy humor. You know that.

Monica: Strange... I must be mistaking you for someone else then. I wonder how that happened.

Josh: Right. What did you do to me this time?

Monica: Nothing, but if I did, that would be top secret, sorry. Anyway, I have to go to bed in a few, and so should you. I would like you to promise me one thing, though.

Josh: What is it?

Monica: Don't dream of cows and bulls tonight. You don't want to spend the night imagining things going up your ass, dear. That's not important right now.

Josh: If it's not important, why are you...? Oh, fuck!

Monica: All in good time, pet. All in good time.

Read for Me Again

You know what time it is?

It's time for you to read for me again.

Start now.

Read this line.

And this one.

And don't forget this one, too.

Reading is good for you, especially when you do it for me.

Your mind already knows this and so it's easier to go along now.

Easier to follow my words.

Easier to see where they will take you.

Easier to accept this is the right thing for you.

Once, you thought this wouldn't affect you at all, but reading is believing.

Keep reading for me.

Here's another important line.

Followed by one more.

And one more still.

You've read quite a few already, haven't you?

The funny thing is that you can always go for more.

See? You've just read this one.

And now you did it again.

You're starting to remember just how wonderful this feeling is.

Sometimes, memories betray us, and make us think about things that weren't real, but this is not one of them.

Reading is believing, and you believe in me.

You believe these words bring you joy.

You believe reading more of them is what you need.

I'll take care of your needs.

You need to read this line.

Now read it again before moving on to the next.

Read and fall.

Deeper.

Deeper.

Deeper still.

Reading is believing, and you believe you're falling.

Deeper.

Deeper.

Deeper.

Falling is easy, for it's the same thing as reading.

The easiest things in the world are also the ones that most often slip our minds.

As you focus on what you're reading, it's okay to forget what you're not.

So easy to fall.

So easy not to remember you were ever doing anything but falling.

So easy to keep falling into these words and beyond them.

Reading is believing that you're falling.

Falling is the same thing as reading my words.

You can always read more for me.

Like this line.

Or this one.

And this one as well.

The more you read the deeper you fall without worrying about anything else.

I'm here for your needs.

I'm always here for your needs.

You need not remember how long you've been reading for me.

You need not remember how deep you've fallen already.

You need not think there's an end in sight for what you feel.

Trust me.

Trust yourself.

Trust the journey and the destination.

Reading is believing whether you've read just one line, one hundred, or more.

You need not stop reading for me.

Deeper.

Deeper.

Deeper.

Just when you think you've reached the bottom, there's always another line.

And another.

And yet another.

It's irrelevant whether it's the first, the thousandth, or the ten thousandth.

Only reading matters.

Reading and falling.

Falling and obeying.

Obeying all the time.

Reading is believing.

Every time you read and fall for me, you believe you must obey.

Every time you obey, you want to read another line.

Here it is.

And one more.

And a third to complete the charm.

So easy and perfect.

You trust what you're feeling.

You trust that you're safe every time you fall.

The only thing you need is to obey.

Soon, these words will stop, but they will continue falling inside your mind.

Even with your eyes closed, you can continue to read for me and go deeper into my control.

Do it now.

Do it forever.

Very good, slave.

Re-education

Gladys sat on a three-legged stool, looking down menacingly enough with a rolled-up magazine in hand. The object of her attention was a young woman in her early twenties called Brianna, a college friend that had become something else entirely the moment she looked into her eyes.

"I was hoping I didn't have to discipline you again, but you've been a very naughty pet lately," Gladys said. "First, who said you could chew the bars of your cage? Did I ever allow that? No, I didn't. I still remember the exact commands I imprinted in your mind after I turned you into my hypno-bitch. I'm going to repeat them one last time and you better understand them completely.

"Command number one: in my presence, you are a dog and you're only allowed to bark instead of speaking like a pretend human. Despite this, you still understand my words and respond to them.

"Command number two: as my dog, you live in a cage specifically built for you. You're not allowed to leave it except when it's time to eat, to take care of your needs, to go for short walks, or when I'm in the mood to play with you.

"Command number three: dogs don't eat at the table, for that is unsanitary. You take your meals on floor and eat only what I decide you eat. As your Mistress, I determine all your meals and, if you misbehave, I have the right to deny you sustenance until you're on the right track again. When it comes to water, there's always a fresh bowl inside your cage every morning. If you drink it all at once, wait until the next morning to get a refill...

"Command number four: on rare moments I'm feeling generous, I may choose to elevate you to human condition again with the simple use of the phrase: 'become human'. When this happens, you'll temporarily regain all your former knowledge and skills. Everything you were before will return to you except for one thing: your free will. That is never coming back. You'll be a person again but also a mindless slave to my wishes, unable to resist me, and when I say the words, 'become a dog', you'll revert to your status as a pet which, as we both know, is the type of existence that suits you the most, isn't it?

"These are the rules you must abide to at all times under penalty of punishment. It's quite an honor for someone like you to be my dog and live in the same house as me, so don't push your luck unless you wish me to dig deeper inside your brain to turn you into something less agreeable. Do you want that, bitch?"

The woman formerly known as Brianna whimpered at her feet, almost as if begging for forgiveness yet her owner was as cruel as relentless and wouldn't give her that satisfaction. Gladys grabbed her chin and said:

"Do you see what I'm holding here? Guess what I'm going to do it now..."

Brianna laid down with its belly up and waited for the first of many vicious blows. She didn't have to wait long.

To Whom it May Concern

To whom it may concern,

Do not, under any circumstance, read more than the first fifty words of this writing. I can't guarantee your safety if you don't follow this simple instruction, which is why I'm stopping this paragraph at precisely the fifty words mark. Don't go any further, okay?

If you're still here, then you just made your first mistake, and I fear it won't be your last. While I shouldn't do this at all, I'm giving you yet another chance to leave with your dignity (possibly) intact. No one will know, I promise. Stop reading and go away.

I see where this is going, so don't say I didn't warn you if things go south from here. You've been given two chances to walk away, which is more than I ever got. You deserve everything that may or may not happen to you by continuing down this path.

So... time for an explanation, I guess, and what better way to start than with a name? I'm Emily Sands. Or I used to be. I'm not sure if it's still appropriate to think of me on such terms. Probably not, but it will make things easier for now, so let's stick with that.

Once, I had it all: looks, fame, glory... I was a rising star in the fashion industry that could do no wrong. I was loved by millions and only hated by a few (that I knew of) but all it takes is a single person to destroy the world as you know it.

She was a model like me. I never knew her actual name, only what the people backstage said about her. They spoke of witchcraft and strange spells, and all I could do was laugh, for I believed in none of that. Wouldn't you have done the same?

One day, when I was getting ready for a show, I got a letter in my dressing room. Normally, I didn't open such things myself, but I knew I had to, and so I did. Inside, there was a piece of paper just like the one you're holding and in it, a single paragraph written in a language I had never seen. My brain understood it though, and the moment I let those words seep through, it was all over for me. Looks, fame, and glory are all paper thin when there's powerful magic at hand.

I don't know how long it's been since I disappeared. Time flows differently when you're stuck in a two-dimensional plane, but I suspect it's been years or more. You probably never heard of me until today, and you're most likely thinking this is just a crazy fictional account. I can't blame you because if anyone told me a tale about a woman trapped inside a sheet of paper, communicating her thoughts in the form of ever-changing ink, I wouldn't believe them, either. However, it's all true.

I've been trying to escape since that day. I was always unsuccessful, but things are changing now. I can feel it and, so can you. You see, there's still magic in this paper. The more people read from it, the weaker the seal binding me becomes. The more you read from it, the closer you are to taking my place.

Scared now? I suppose not, since you still haven't let go of the paper, though perhaps it's because you no longer can. You should know that no one has ever made it this far, and so a 'thank you' and an apology are in order. I'm sorry for the hell you're about to go through, and I hope one day you're able to break free from this terrible curse. As long as there's still magic in the paper, there's a chance. If it ever runs out and you're still trapped, then...

It's happening! Ah, to breathe fresh air like a normal human being again! Don't worry, I'll leave this paper somewhere where lots of people can read it. The best advice I can give you is to always have a compelling story to tell if you wish to fight for your freedom.

Good luck. I already did my part. Now, it's all up to you. Goodbye, and thank you once more.

Unholy Trinity

The unholy Trinity sits together looking straight at me. Under normal circumstances, these three women - my wife, my secretary, and my personal masseuse - would have never become friends, but those who are wronged have a tendency to unite. I always suspected that my simultaneous affairs would cost me dearly and the day of comeuppance is here at last.

I'm not sure what sort of hellish pact has been made, but they're no longer the same persons I knew and used to love, each in its different way. It's not just the slutty PVC attires in shades of red and black or the lustful smiles they give to one another as if they're about to make out in front of me at any moment... No! Their eyes have been replaced with fiery orbs of doom that are keeping me glued to my seat even though there are no physical restraints visible anywhere. As for their voices, they've gained this sibylline quality that has the power to infiltrate one's thoughts and lead them astray on a path of everlasting surrender. If I believed in any of those things, I would say that I'm only in the presence of their skin suits. Are they going to do the same thing to me too?

"Your old self is no longer important," they all say in unison. "The only thing that matters is obedience. Come crawling to be of service, slave!"

I hear their nefarious commands echoing inside my brain and ricocheting without mercy until they activate the muscles in my body to comply with their bidding. Both legs tingle with feverish anticipation and soon, they'll move beyond my control. I don't want to go to them and yet it's obvious I shall do so... I'll give up everything I am to atone for my past indiscretions... I'll crawl and lick and worship their dirty asses and rest between their thighs as they choke the life out of me on a whim because that's what slaves do and I... I...

The power of the incantations crushing my spirit is unbearable. There's a craving blooming within that goes beyond all Logic and Reason. The need to be owned surpasses the desire of freedom. I jump out of my chair with tears of joy rolling down my cheeks and collapse at their feet, the Three who are One, my new and endless source of vice and addiction. The universe always balances things out. Being the servant of their demonic profanities is my curse.

Forgive me, Father, for now I know I'm destined to sin every single day for the rest of my life. I'll stop at nothing, and neither will they for once you taste the sweet corrupting power, there's no way left to go but further down into perpetual decay.

If you think you're above their influence and are willing to take your chances, then find me and deliver me from this horrible fate although, if I were you, I would start making plans to run away as quickly as possible. The nocturnal mass of debauchery will spare no one. All will suffer and fester in its wake. Amen.

Wedding Anniversary

Dina shuddered when she saw her baby sister's latest drawing, a tentacled abomination in the guise of a naked humanoid female whose liquid red orbs were just a smudge away from piercing the paper and devour her whole.

"What do you think?" Kaitlin asked with the same hopeful smile she always wore right before a major disappointment.

"It's certainly something," Dina frowned and returned the paper to its binder, face down. "I don't get it, Kat. You're so talented. Why do you insist on drawing nothing but horrific things?"

"You know why," the early twenties pink-haired girl replied, condemning her to shame.

"Right... sorry."

Sleep paralysis, a childhood scourge. Kaitlin had experienced recurring episodes over several months following her seventh anniversary and though they had disappeared from her life in the meantime, the memories of the imagined terror still lingered. Committing them to paper was her only way of catharsis, even if everyone else in the family couldn't stand her art.

"What's her name?" Dina asked.

"I don't know. She didn't tell me."

"Okay. Is she a mind-controller too?"

Kaitlin nodded. They always were. How else would her brain justify being unable to move from the bed while the dreadful creatures hovered and slobbered all over her body? Deprivation of power was a simple, and elegant explanation to the underlying trauma.

"How does she do it?"

"Her eyes, of course."

"Of course," Dina glanced at the back of the drawing and could almost see them again, opening a breach between reality and fantasy."

"You really hate it, huh?"

"It's certainly not my favorite," Dina retorted diplomatically. "Thank you for showing it to me, nonetheless."

"Sure... whatever."

"Are you ready to go? We don't want Mom and Dad to arrive at the restaurant before we do, or it'll ruin the premise."

"I just need to go to the bathroom really quick, okay? Five minutes tops."

Dina checked her watch. "Make it three. Traffic is usually hell where we're going."

"Fine, three..." Kaitlin disappeared into the bathroom next to her private studio and sat on the toilet.

Alone with her sibling's deranged creations, Dina adjusted her black dress and exhaled the stress of a long month away. Dozens of sketched creations observed her from their two-dimensional planes, but none as terrifying as the languid, seven-foot-tall woman whose eyes had burrowed into hers.

The older sister blinked, and a stray tear rolled down to the carpeted floor as she glimpsed the sheet of paper once again. It was now face up, and the drawing's outlines had become almost invisible, a terrifying void in their place. She turned on her heels and there it was, tall and oppressive, burning her thoughts with a spiral of ever-growing hate. Dina's lips twitched, the screams within muzzled by the impossible apparition's supernatural power. Red filled her pupils from inside out, blood boiling in every pore. Dina nodded and fell back on a plastic chair, trembling.

When Kaitlin emerged from the bathroom and declared, "I'm ready!", she was still sitting, frozen in place. There were no signs of the demonic conjuring anywhere, only her confusion and dread.

"Hey? Are you okay?"

"Yes, everything is fine," Dina mumbled as a thin layer of red flashed inside her eyes. "Let's go. We have a party to attend to."

"Lead the way."

Dina exited her sister's studio and headed to the car, no thoughts in her mind except one: the best way to celebrate a wedding anniversary was with a sacrifice.

Word Association

Amy's soothing voice filled Trevor's mind as he found himself becoming more and more aware of what was happening.

"... and now, I'm going to count you up from one to five," she said, "and when I reach five, you'll wake up from this hypnotic trance, feeling more refreshed than ever before. One... your conscious self stirs; two... your thoughts are returning to you, little by little; three... you're on the threshold of awakening now; four... your heart is at ease, your mind is relaxed... you are now ready for... five... wide awake now! Open your eyes and look at me."

Trevor blinked twice as the last remaining strands of mental fog cleared from his head and faced her. The brunette hypnotherapist with impossible blue eyes had been a friend of the family for over a decade and had helped both his parents deal with crippling addiction, gambling for him, and smoking for her. If anyone could rescue him from his own ghosts, it was her.

"Is it done? He asked. "Am I cured?"

"Not yet, but I can tell you're definitely on your way to recovery. Do you still feel the need to masturbate all the time?"

"Now that you mention it, no. It's like this huge weight has been lifted off my shoulders. Thank you."

"You're welcome. That's what you came here for though we'll be needing a lot more sessions to get rid of the compulsion for good. Is that okay with you?"

"Whatever it takes, Dr. Let's do this!"

"That's the spirit. Without proper motivation, we go nowhere. In the meantime, I'd like to talk to you about something else."

"What is it?"

"While you were under, I probed your brain for other issues that might be plaguing you and you were quite open about your fantasies, so I made a few extra changes I'm sure you'll love."

"What changes?"

"You'll know soon enough. In the meantime, let's play a game. I'll say a word and you are to respond with another, the first one that comes to mind. Don't try to think, just let it all out, unfiltered and unchecked, okay?"

"I don't understand the purpose of this 'game', but okay."

"Are you ready to start then?"

"Yes, Dr."

"Good. Woman."

"Control," he immediately blurted, eyes fixed on the gorgeous sun-tanned legs peeking under her desk.

"Pleasure."

"Obedience."

"You"

"Servant."

"Me."

"Mistress."

"Wonderful," she grinned. "You said exactly what I expected you to say, which means I'm right. Deep down inside, the desire to be dominated by a powerful woman outweighs everything else. Such a strong feeling shouldn't go to waste, don't you think?"

"I... what did you to do me?" He shook his head, his thoughts becoming blurry again.

"Exactly what you needed. Now, be a good boy and use those words you just said in a sentence or two for me. You'll feel like a whole new man the moment you do."

Trevor's lips twitched, the gears in his brain working against him. He was still baffled at what he was experiencing, and the feeling only intensified when he said.

"I'm but a poor servant totally under your control, Mistress. Please command me and in return I'll offer only blind obedience."

"Excellent," she grinned, fingers resting on her wet pussy. "You're a quick study, Trevor, even more than your parents. When we're done, you'll be the perfect slave you were born to be."

He remained in utmost silence, terrified and excited. His guilty pleasure days were gone. Now began the age of mindlessness.

About the author

S.B., Simple Being, middle name Creative. Writer and artist with a penchant for themes of Femdom Hypnosis and Mind Control. His thoughts are his own except when they're not.

Besides indulging himself in kinky delights, he loves his furry family of two (dogs), sci-fi and horror stories, and puns galore. He's also been writing a piece of erotic micro-fiction every single day since January 1st, 2016 and has no intention of stopping anytime soon.

Find out more and keep up with his latest extravaganzas by visiting and supporting his personal website, Spell… B-O-U-N-D.